When I First Held You

A Lullaby from Israel

Mirik Snir  Eleyor Snir

KAR-BEN
PUBLISHING

On the day
you were born

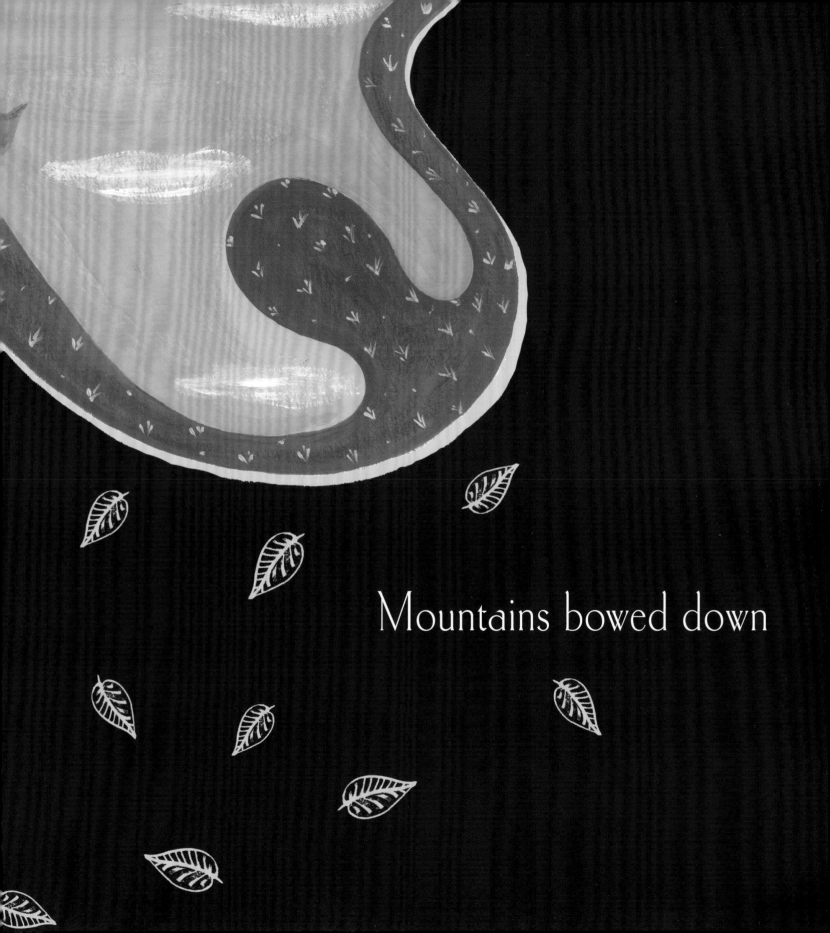

Mountains bowed down

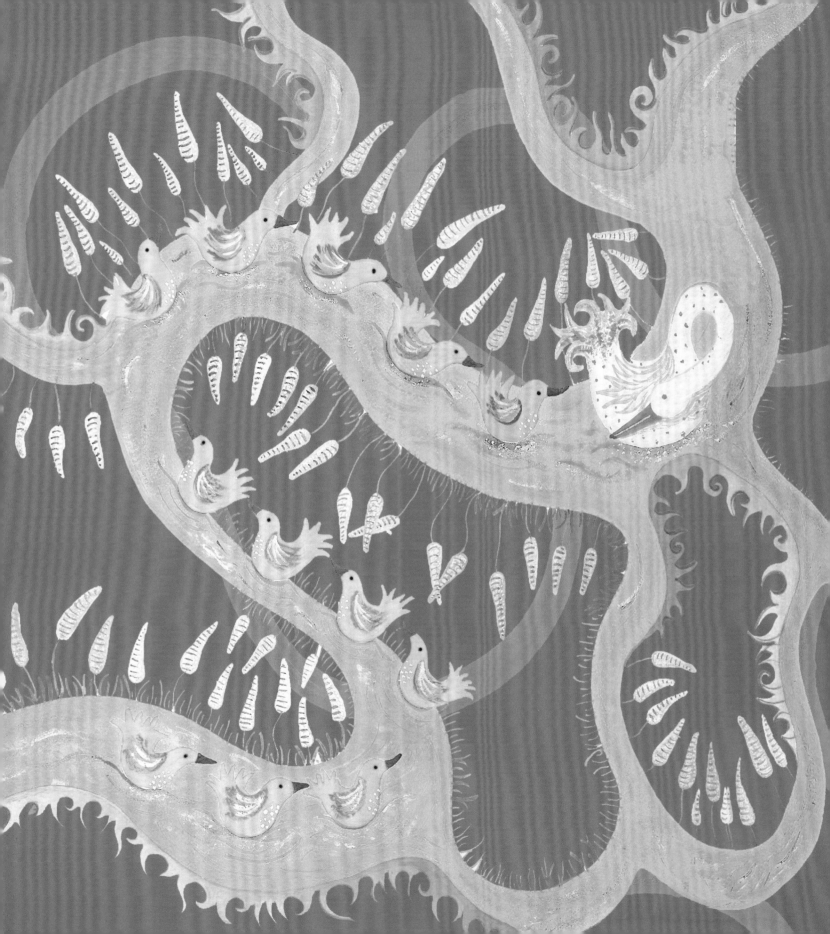

Rivers ran 'round

Trees were drumming

Flowers strumming

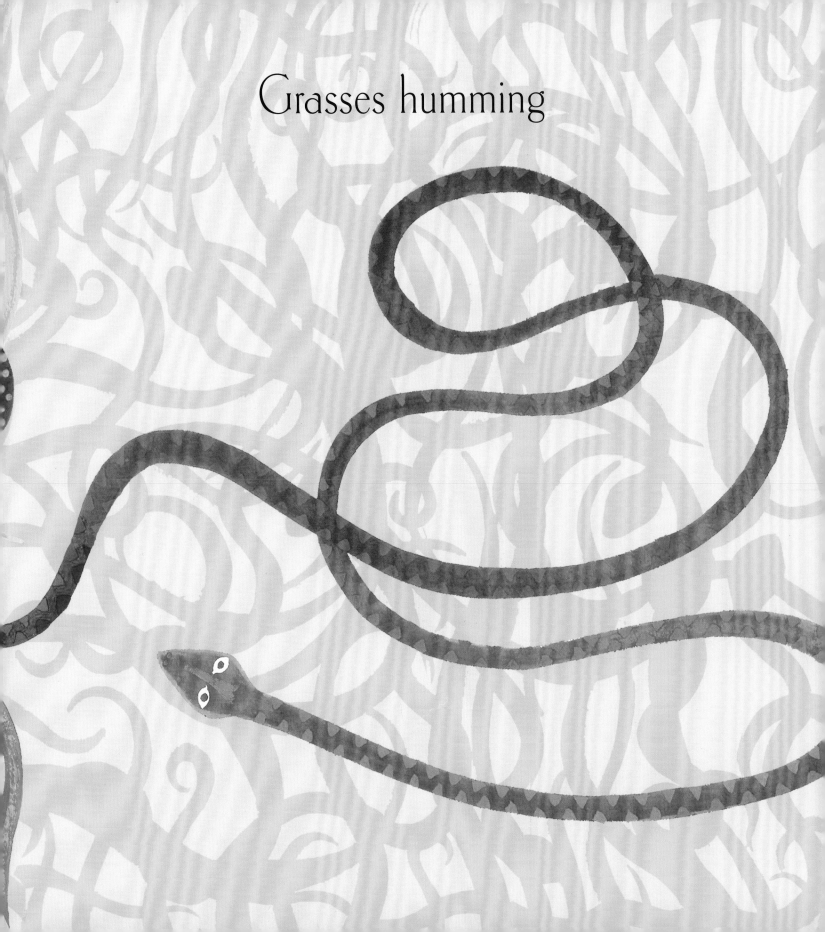

Grasses humming

Winds caressed

Moonlight blessed

Clouds danced above

Sunbeams sent love

Rain tapped a song

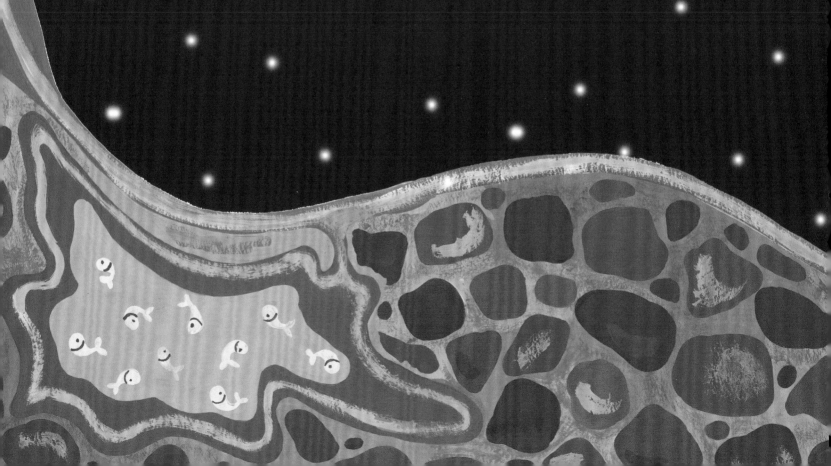

Rocks rolled along

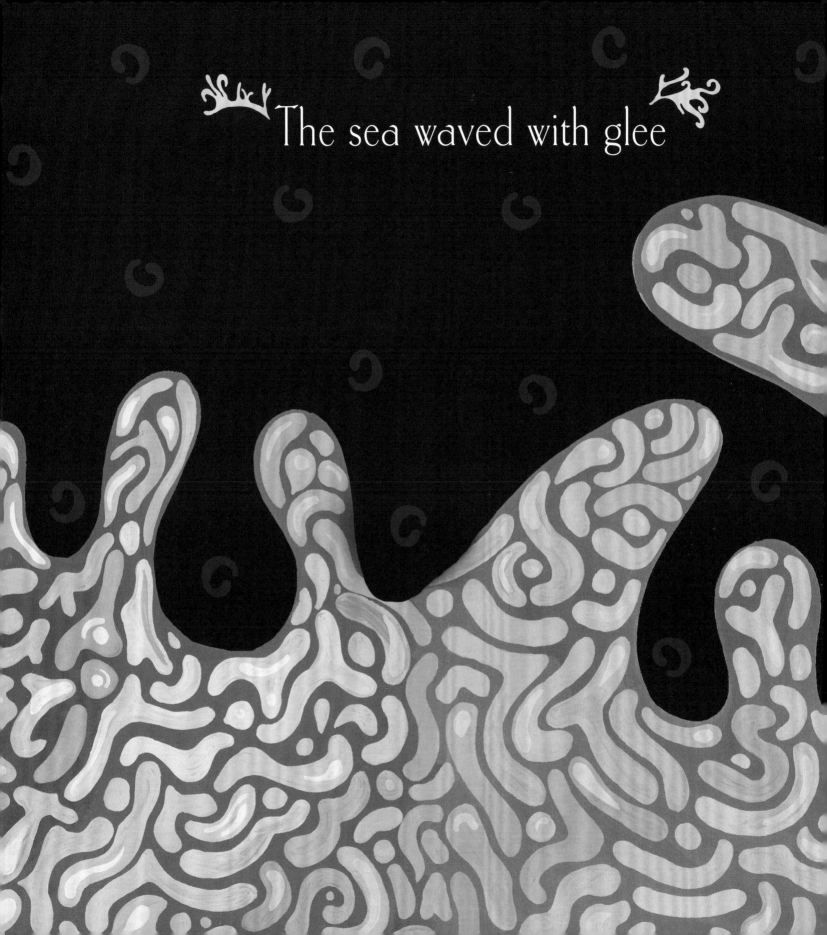

The sea waved with glee

When I held you
close to me

Place your child's photo here

The Day You Were Born

"הַיּוֹם בּוֹ נוֹלַדְתָּ
הוּא הַיּוֹם בּוֹ הֶחֱלִיט הקב"ה
שֶׁהָעוֹלָם אֵינוֹ יָכוֹל לְהִתְקַיֵּים בִּלְעָדֶיךָ"

רבי נחמן מברסלב.

The day you were born is the
day God decided that the world
could not exist without you.

—Rabbi Nachman of Breslov

KAR-BEN PUBLISHING INC.
A division of Lerner Publishing Group, Inc.
241 First Avenue North
Minneapolis, MN 55401
1-800-4KARBEN

Website address: www.kar-ben.com

Library of Congress Cataloging-in-Publication Data

Snir, Mirik
    When I first held you : a lullaby from Israel / by Mirik Snir ; illustrated by Eleyor Snir; translated from the Hebrew by
Mary Jane Shubow.
        p.   cm
    Summary: A parent describes, in rhyming text, the beauty of the world on the day a young child is born.
    ISBN 978-0-7613-5096-5 (lib. bdg. : alk. paper)
    [1. Stories in rhyme. 2. Mother and child—Fiction. 3. Nature—Fiction. 4. Lullabies.] I. Snir, Eleyor. II. Shubow,
Mary Jane. III. Title.
    PZ8.3.S67265Wh 2009
    [E]—dc22   2008053741

Manufactured in the United States of America
3 — PC — 12/13/11